Fairy Tales Can Come True

THE BEGINNING

Written and Illustrated

by

LINDA GUNN

ISBN: 979-8-8690-4411-2   (Paperback Edition)
ISBN: 979-8-8690-4740-3   (Hardcover Edition)
ISBN: 979-8-8690-4742-7   (E-book Edition)

Some characters and events in this book are fictitious and products of the author's imagination. Any similarity to real persons, living or dead, is coincidental and not intended by the author.

BOOK ONE

THE PRETEND

Love is an attempt to change a piece of a dream—world
into reality.

Henry David Thoreau

I want to share these events from my childhood with others who secretly believe in their happiest dreams, because there are times in life when the imagined really does become reality.

PREFACE

"Seagully, I'm supposed to be in swim class, but I hate trying to keep up with the class. Besides, why would I want to spend my time in the water trying not to drown when I can sit out here with you? You are always waiting for me on your buoy. I'd sit next to you instead of on this rope if I could get up there without the buoy tipping. Are you really a bird? Let's pretend that you are Peter Pan in a bird body. What a neat thought! You could come to my house late some night and take me to Neverland!

CHAPTER ONE

Dreams that are never imagined can never come true.

Fern Bowen

Nina shivers in the shade of the tall building while waiting for the 8:00 a.m. bus to Alamitos Bay. Today is the last Friday of summer vacation. Next week she'll start 5th grade. Before that, though, she has to take the swim test that she has managed to avoid for weeks. She hides under her beach towel, hoping she can shut out thoughts of the dreaded test. Her younger sister, Mo, relentlessly teases her.

"You think you are going to drown!" Mo chants, poking fun at her.

Aggravated, Nina pulls her beach towel even closer, thinking that Mo might be right. Nina knows she can stay afloat for hours on end, but she never has been able to swim fast for a long distance. She didn't participate as she should have in this summer's swim class to learn the proper way to swim because she didn't want to have to put her face in the water. Maybe she'll get so tired that she'll sink to her death!

For the past three summers, Nina and her older sister Marie have advanced through the Red Cross Swim Program at Alamitos Bay. Marie passed the Advanced Swimmer test during the second week of vacation this year. She does everything well (except for being part of the family!). She plays the harmonica, the piano, and the cello, and is a good student in school.

Unlike Marie, Nina spent her hours at the bay this summer daydreaming while sitting out on the rope between two buoys that mark the swim area. It's a great place to be alone, even if the rope is slimy with long green moss! She's made good use of her time living in an Imaginary world, but hasn't improved her swimming skills.

Nina is not a good student, does not pay attention in class, and enjoys making people laugh by acting silly. Her musical ability is limited to simple songs that she plays on the piano with her index finger. She taunts her sisters by playing and singing made-up songs with secret name-calling lyrics. In fact, that's where the nickname "Mo" came from that everyone calls her younger sister, Marta.

Nina's worst made-up name of all time is "Mocoso." That name means everything bad in the whole wide world to anyone Nina says it to, but it means everything good if anybody says it to her. Marta went berserk every time Nina called her that when she first came up with it, so she was dubbed "Mo" forever. Mo tried to make up her own evil name to call Nina, but Nina said that no name could replace Mocoso, and any name Mo called her would only mean something good!

There are two things that Nina can do well—housework, and obeying her mother (who, by the way, is not aware that Nina has not taken this summer's Advanced Swimmer class, so there is no way for Nina to avoid today's test).

Unfortunately, Nina's favorite pastime of daydreaming while sitting on a wet bus bench won't make her swim test go away. "If the bus crashes before it gets to this stop, I might be late to the bay and miss the test," she thinks to herself. "Or maybe Mom will forget about my swim test. Nah, fat chance that would ever happen!"

As Nina silently hopes in vain, Mo turns her teasing comments toward her oldest sister, Marie. Poor Marie. She hates to be seen with her mother and sisters. It's bad enough that she is responsible for her younger sisters when Mom is away or busy, but to spend the whole summer with them has been torture. Marie can be mean to Mo, so it comes as no surprise when Marie slugs the little pest in the stomach.

When Mo is hurt, everybody for miles around can hear her wail. This morning's wail seems to echo off the surrounding buildings and bounce back to all three girls. Mom is quick to jump to her youngest daughter's defense, and both Nina and Marie are scolded.

Much to Nina's disappointment, the bus arrives.

THE SWIM TEST...

This morning the tide in the bay is unusually high, leaving little room to spread out the beach blanket and provisions. Nina usually loves high tides, but not today.

The ramp to the float appears to be coming out of the water. She wades the hesitation in ankle deep water to the four steps at the foot of the ramp. The north side of the float is crowded with other swimmers her age. They are awaiting the instructor's whistle – the signal to dive into the cold water.

TWEEEEET!

The shrill whistle penetrates Nina's whole being as she runs to get in line. Late as usual (but not late enough), she watches the class dive head first off the float to start their mile swimm to the Second Street bridge. She jumps off the edge of the float while holding her nose. Not being bouyant, her skinny body shoots straight down like an arrow. She has a fleeting memory of the time she almost drowned when Marie tricked her into jumping in once before, believing that the water around the foot of the float was not deep.

This time the shock of the cold water is just as horrible! She kicks hard to rise to the surface and emerges gasping for air. All she can see of the class is the splashing of their paddling feet. She starts swimming with her face out of the water, at record speed for all of half a minute. Then she swims the sidestroke on her right side until she gets tired, and turns over to do the sidestroke on her left side. Five minutes pass. and Nina is out of breath and tired, Mo's words echo in her head.

"You think you are going to drown!"

Fear and panic take hold as she realizes that she does not have enough strength to make it all the way to the Second Street bridge. She rolls over on her back and floats. "Floating is a good way for a tired swimmer to rest," her Beginning Swimmer instructor always said. The one thing she can do well in the water Is float. She set the record as the longest floater in her Beginning Swimmer class. The trick to floating is to keep your head back and your belly button out of the water. She practices floating in the bathtub, although it's not easy any more because she has grown.

This morning's sky resembles a seascape. Some of the windswept clouds appear to be rolling surf, and Nina imagines that she is flying over the ocean. Her Imagination is keen enough for her to pretend that her world is upside down.

She sings,

"Think of the happiest things, it's the same as having wings… you can fly, you can fly, you can fly."

Water floods her mouth, and she rights herself while coughing. Her seagull friend has landed close by.

"Hi Seagully! Bet you wondered why I'm not sitting on the rope. I'm supposed to be taking this stupid swim test. I'm glad nobody knows that I'm part of the class, because I will never catch up. I wish there was a test for roller skating or doing fancy tricks while riding my bike. I would impress everybody, because I am the best!"

Nina is by far the best skater on her block. She climbs trees and street signposts while wearing her skates because it would be a waste of time to take them off. Besides, she might need to make a fast getaway once she is on the ground.

She also performs ballet-like positions while standing on her bicycle seat, she can twirl two Hula Hoops at once, and she is an expert on her Pogo Stick.

She says to Seagully, "You are so lucky to fly wherever you want to go. If I could fly, I would fly low over the swim class. Wouldn't that surprise them! Then I would fly away to Neverland and be Peter Pan's best friend. I would be his new Wendy. The old Wendy died a hundred years ago, so he surely must be ready for some adventures with a new sidekick — me! I've been wondering. Is flying like floating on the water, only upside down?"

Nina has spent this summer talking to her seagull friend, who usually sits on the buoy that is attached to the slimy rope. She shares her lunch with him, singing and telling him stories. Seagully is being very patient waiting for his bit of sandwich. Finally, seeing that she has no food, he flies away.

Nina continues floating and imagines that she has drowned and become a mermaid.

Looking toward shore, she can see Mo running across people's blankets and smashing through a sand castle. Nobody ever gets mad at her no matter what she does because she is so cute.

"I wonder where Marie Is?'

Nina guesses that Marie is watching the high school boys performing stunts on the high rings. Because she is tall for her age, Marie thinks that she looks grown up enough to pretend that she is in high school. All she cares about are boys, clothes, and her hair. She has lost her imagination, her sense of humor, and no longer seems to care about being Nina's best friend. Nina misses the fun times spent with her big sister, who used to sing to her and share her adventures from Campfire Girls Camp. Things are sure different now.

Nina begins kicking her feet while lying on her back. It's a fast and easy way to move across the water except that you can't see where you are going. After kicking for what seems like a long time, she stops and treads water to get her bearings. She is surprised to see how much distance she has covered. Actually, the swift current has helped propel her across the water and she is not far from the Second Street bridge. She can see the rest of the class on the beach, gathered around the instructor, who is giving them their Red Cross cards. Relieved that nobody has noticed her, she pretends to swim just in case someone looks her way.

Finally, she reaches the red buoy that marks the swim area next to the bridge. The beach looks very far away even though the tide is receding, but knowing that the shallow water is close, she treads water moving forward toward shore until she feels the soft sandy bottom with the tips of her toes. Her legs are wobbly as she climbs out of the water.

The beach is deserted except for Mom, who is waiting with Nina's towel.

"I'm so proud of you! You passed the Advanced Swimmer test!" Mom says as she hands Nina a card with her name on it.

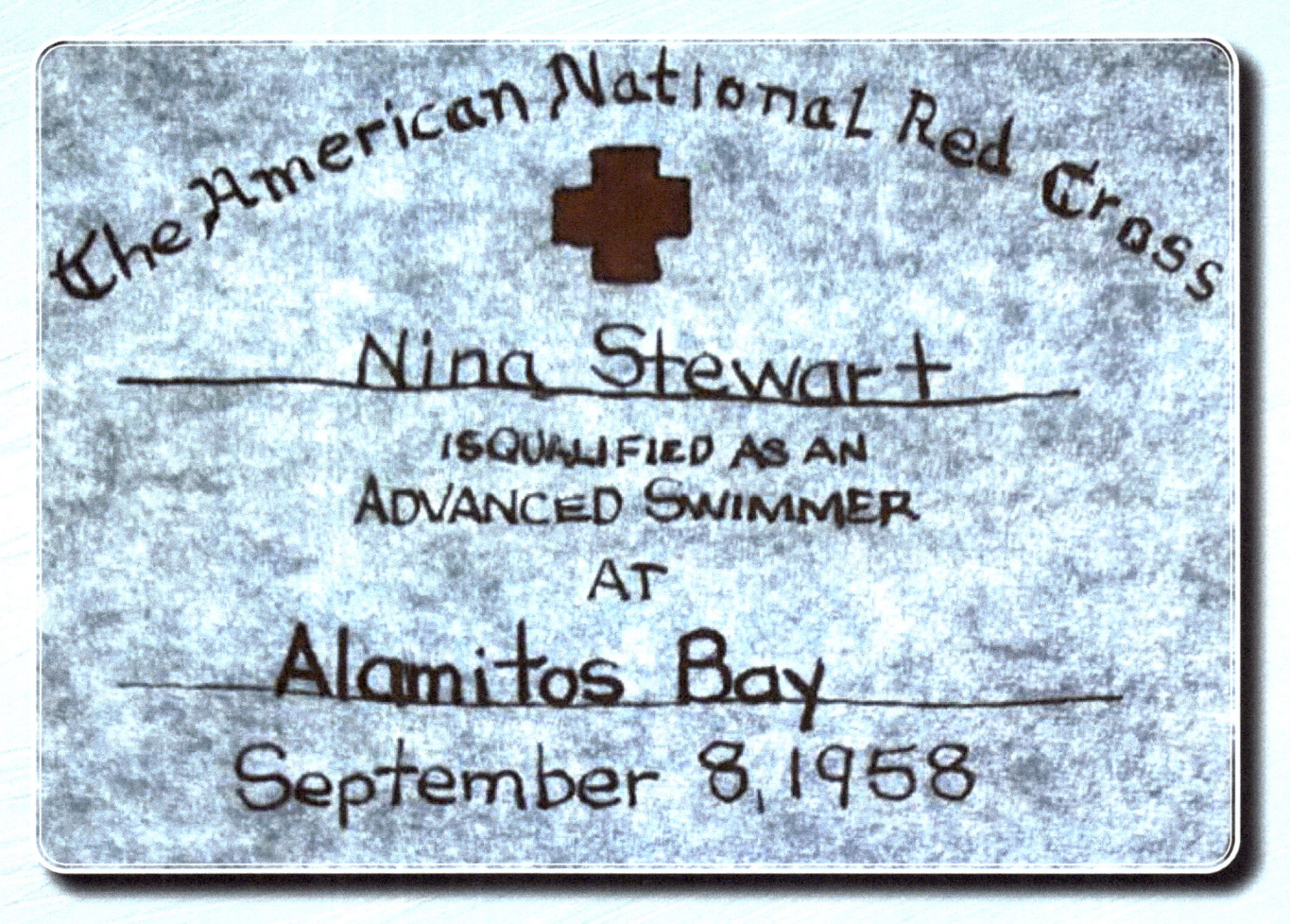

The American National Red Cross

Nina Stewart

IS QUALIFIED AS AN
ADVANCED SWIMMER
AT

Alamitos Bay

September 8, 1958

Nina mutters under her breath , "I didn't swim all the way."

She wonders if the instructor even saw her jump off the float to take the test. More than likely, Mom just asked him to make a card for her floating her daughter. Oh, well. At least the test is over and she won't ever have to do that again (she hopes).

CHAPTER TWO

We are the music—makers,
And we are the dreamers of dreams...

Arthur O. Shaughnessy

Nina can feel the glares as she sits between Marie and Mo in the back seat of the car. They have just been scolded by Mom for pinching and pulling each other's hair. Mom always has Nina sit between her sisters when they fight. Nina quickly dismisses today's tension. Her thoughts are on the music playing on the radio.

"Fairy tales can come true. It can happen to you.

If you're young at heart."

She is thrilled to hear an adult confirming her secret beliefs – and on the radio no less!

Nina's dad often comments that her head is in the clouds, but she does know the difference between her daydreams and reality, and knows in her heart that sometimes the imagined can become reality. She is excited to think that something wonderful is about to happen and sings to herself,

"When you wish upon a star, makes no difference who you are.

Anything your heart desires will come to you…"

The song on the radio and this, her favorite song, confirm in her young mind that at least one of her daydreams, fantasies, or wishes will come true. After all, she has a young heart like in the song and never plans to stop imagining.

Marie just stares at her singing sister in disgust.

CABRILLIO BEACH…

Nina and her sisters love to follow Dad as he explores Cabrillo Beach. The first place he routinely leads his family to is the break wall where the girls leap from one large flat rock to another. Their quest is to see how far out from the beach they can venture before the threat of being washed off the wall by a powerful wave or, to be more realistic, a stern request from Mom, turns them back toward the beach. If only they could make it to the end of the wall to explore the inside of the lighthouse. That's not likely to happen because it's too dangerous to venture that far along the wall. Besides that, it must be at least a mile long to the end!

Dad reminds and warns again, "Just last week another fisherman was washed off these rocks, and his buddy slipped on wet moss and fell into one of these deep crevasses. SLOW DOWN AND WATCH WHERE YOU LEAP!"

The gaps between the rocks grow wider as the wall veers away from the beach. Nina looks in every crack for remains of the lost fisherman. Some of the crevasses contain pieces of dead tree branches, spider webs, and crabs that scamper sideways down into the bottomless depths. There is no trace of anything human other than snagged fishing line, a candy bar wrapper, and a very old Coke bottle. The huge rocks are stacked carefully from the ocean floor to rise several feet above the water, and they extend almost a mile. The rocks that form the top of the wall have been hewn into giant rectangles. Even though they were carefully placed to form a flat surface with a tight fit, many have been dislodged and have shifted due to the storms that have battered the wall, leaving gaps large enough for a man to fall into. The mostly flat surface makes running and leaping impossible to resist, giving Dad good cause to be forceful in his warning to Mo and Nina.

Nina calls back to Dad, "Did they find the dead bodies?"

"No. It's been speculated that their bodies were washed out to the sea," he replies.

Nina wonders why the bodies were never found and says, "I think they were eaten by a sea monster! Otherwise their bodies would have washed up on the beach."

"Get real!" snaps Marie.

"YOU GET REAL! What else would have happened to them?" Nina snaps back at her know–it–all big sister.

"Now girls," says Mom. "Let's not bicker. We're here to enjoy the day."

Mo is now standing in front of what used to be a chain link fence that was erected to deter people from venturing out to the end of the wall. The rusty supports and fencing have been twisted and torn in a way that no longer makes it a barrier.

"Wow!" says Nina. "Look! The break wall has been broken here!"

She squeezes through the fence and climbs on her hands and knees over a torn sandbag. Mo is right behind her, but there are very deep gaps between the steep jagged rocks that make it impossible for the two girls to safety continue their quest.

It is no surprise to hear Mom's stern reprimand, "That's far enough! It's time to go back now."

"OH PLEASE, can't we go just a little bit farther? We'll be careful not to fall," Nina pleads.

Mo turns around and quickly climbs back through the fence on her hands and knees, then gets up to begin her running and leaping back over the flat rocks. She wants to be the first one back to the picnic table, but Nina, who always wins every race, teasingly nudges past her little sister chanting, "You can't beat me!"

Nina's little nudge is more like of a slight push, and causes Mo to slip on a moss-covered rock and fall to her knees.

"Here it comes," says Marie while holding her hands tightly over her ears.

She had lagged behind the family hoping to look like a lone hiker. However, Mo and Nina turned around and ran in her direction in their race, they had almost reached her when Mo fell.

A mortified Marie tries to distance herself from them before Mo starts screaming, but it's too late. Mo's piercing wails are already drawing attention from everyone within hearing distance, including the cute lifeguard. There is no escape for the embarrassed Marie, who shouts back at Mom, "This is the last time I will go anywhere with you guys!"

Nina does not understand why her big sister is so angry and says to Mom, "She doesn't like us, does she?"

Mom's answer is not what Nina expects to hear. "Marie is growing up, just as you and Mo will someday."

Nina is adamant in her reply. "I WILL NEVER GROW UP if I have to act like Marie and never have any fun!"

The picnic table is covered in sand, old pine needles, and sticky tree sap, but under Mom's direction, everyone but Dad has to eat lunch at the table. Nina hates to waste time eating when there is exploring to be done. She politely asks, "May I please me excused? I can eat my sandwich while I walk."

As usual, Marie starts complaining," Why should you be excused when we have to sit here? I hate greasy tuna on soggy brown bread!" She rolls her eyes at her smelly sandwich, wraps it in wax paper, and stuffs it into her pocket. Her plan is to feed it to the seagulls.

Dad's loud whistle breaks the tension and Mom relents, "You may all be excused. Your father is waiting to explore the tide pools. Take your sandwiches with you."

An occasional wave ignites gleeful squeals from Mo and Nina as they munch on their sandwiches and maneuver the slippery, narrow trail. They are inching their way around the bluff to the remains of what used to be a house. The girls find that its north–facing wall is half lying on its side. Climbing onto the large chunk of cement will not be easy due to the tidal surge of surf that noisily rumbles over the rocks that separate the path from the wall.

Nina studies their dilemma and loudly says to Mo, "Let me go first. Then I'll help you to the wall."

The surf comes crashing in again, then pulls back, leaving many rocks and pebbles exposed for half a minute before it comes crashing in again. The thrill of danger excites Nina, who quickly but carefully crosses the slippery inlet and inches her way up to the bottom of the wall.

Mo, who did not wait, is standing in the middle of the inlet and gets caught by a larger than usual surge of water. Nina jumps in to help her.

Fear grips them as they are knocked down and pulled over the rocks as the water recedes. Their weightless bodies resemble rag dolls. What a welcome surprise when Dad rushes in and picks up both girls, one under each arm, and carries them to the fallen wall. Nina watches his cigarette bounce in his mouth as he curses, and she wonders what keeps the cigarette from falling out.

A seagull swoops down to pick up Mo's floating tuna sandwich and is joined by three others who screech loudly as they chase after the first one.

Marie, who has no problems crossing over the rocks and getting onto the wall, observes her wet, frightened sisters and asks, "Maybe we can go home now?"

Shivering with cold and bleeding from cuts and scrapes, Nina replies, "I don't want to go home." She loves this part of Cabrillo Beach with its promise of hidden treasures. No way will a little discomfort deter her from this rare adventure!

Mo says, "Remember last year when I stepped on that sea urchin and had to go to the hospital?"

A disgusted Marie glares at her baby sister and hisses, "Yeah, we all had to go to the hospital. Another day wasted."

Mo's encounter with the sea urchin even made the local news. Like a little celebrity, she got presents from just about everyone, just like she did when she had her tonsils taken out.

Mo continues, "I wonder why the Lone Ranger and Tonto weren't there to take out the sea urchin spines. They were there to take my tonsils out"

The fact that Mo would believe just about anything adds to Marie's disgust. How could Mo be so annoying and gullible at the same time?

Dr. Bill had told Mo that he was her TV hero, the masked Lone Ranger with his sidekick, Tonto! And, of course, Mo believed him.

Standing on what once was the floor of the house above the tide pools, Nina spins in a circle with both arms out from her sides and sings to Mo.

"This is my favorite place in the whole wide world because I think that door in the side of the cliff is a secret entrance to Neverland."

Dad appears, followed by Marie, and is quick to shatter Nina's fantasy by abruptly saying, "Stay away from there!"

Mo tells him, "Nina says that door is the secret entrance to Never Neverland."

Marie rolls her eyes again and sighs as she scolds, "Nina has no idea what is behind that door. It's probably just a trash–filled room where a bum sleeps."

Quick to defend herself, Nina calls Marie her worst made up name.

"YOU ARE A BIG FAT MOCOSO!"

Nina's name has no effect on Marie, who shouts back, "Fare may lab ouch!" Marie thinks she's telling Nina to shut up in French, a language she studied in school. Little does she know how badly she massacred what she was trying to say!

Dad, who has kept moving, gives a loud whistle from the tide pools that interrupts the squabble, and the three girls scale down the west side wall to join him, in his explorations.

Nina slips away from the family. Despite her guilt for sneaking away and deliberately disobeying her father, the anticipation of exploring the room behind the mysterious door is worth whatever punishment awaits Nina. The door is cracked open just enough to get a peek inside with one eye. She sees something sparkle and wonders if there is treasure hiding there.

Her curiosity gets the better of her. Using her weight, she pushes open the door. Never has she been so bold! The damp room smells musty and appears to be small.

As Nina's eyes adjust to the darkness, she can see a clean sandy floor and a collection of seashells, rocks, and bird bones that are neatly arranged around the walls. An uneasy feeling that she is invading someone's special place causes her to back toward the door.

Suddenly someone right behind her says, "Don't leave!"

Nina lets out a squeal as she turns to face a barefoot, unusually dressed boy who is grinning at her. His clothes look like they are made of seaweed and seal skin. He has a sheathed knife strapped on his right leg, and his unevenly cut hair Is matted with sand. He has green eyes that seem to sparkle when he smiles at Nina.

The words tumble out of her mouth, "I'd better go. I'm sorry, I didn't know this room was yours."

The boy is standing in front of the door with his hands on his hips. He asks, "Why do you want to leave? You just came in!"

She can't think how she should answer that and nervously says, "because..."

Of course the boy's response is, "Because WHY?"

Nina stutters, "ah... my... my family is looking for me maybe?"

He's not smiling now, and Nina is a little afraid.

He adamantly retorts, "FAMILY! I DON'T NEED ANYBODY TO TELL ME WHAT TO DO OR WHERE TO GO!"

She ignores his remark and changes the subject. "Do you live here? WOW! This is the perfect place. You are so lucky."

He moves away from the door and picks up something sparkly from the corner as Marie's voice can be heard from outside.

"My sister is here. Think I'll scare her!"

The boy is smiling again as Nina pulls open the heavy door and shouts, "BOO!"

Screaming from fright, Marie runs from the door, trips over a rock, and falls. Now the boy is laughing uncontrollably, which makes Nina feel sorry for Marie as she steps out of the little room to show herself. The bright sun makes it hard for her to see Marie, but she can tell by Marie's comment that she's furious!

"YOU ARE REALLY IN TROUBLE NOW!"

Nina excitedly tells Marie, "YOU HAVE TO SEE THE BOY I'VE JUST MET!"

Marie is in no mood for another one of Nina's tall tales. She ignores her request and drags and pulls her by the arm away from the boy in the mysterious room. Dragging her feet all the way, Nina begs, "You have to go back just to look! You have to see the boy who lives there!"

Without a word and jerking hard on Nina's arm, Marie turns and says,

I'll look. But when there is no boy, YOU WILL OWE ME!"

Nina can hardly contain her excitement as Marie pushes open the door. Of course, they find nothing but a smelly, trash–filled room. The boy and his treasures are gone.

"I KNEW IT!" shouts Marie.

Fighting back her tears Nina says, "But there really was a boy in there, and the room was full of things from the ocean!"

Marie argues while pushing her back down the path, "I suppose you want me to believe that it's magic and only you can see it?"

Nina softly answers, "I did see a boy in the room, and it was not full of stinky trash."

Marie was silent for some time before her lecture to Nina. "It's about time for you to grow up and take some responsibility for your actions, and I think that when school starts on Monday, you can walk by yourself. I am in high school now, and I don't need a baby sister tagging behind me.

Nina yells at her, "You are not! You're only in junior high!"

CHAPTER THREE

When your heart is in your dreams, no request is too extreme.

Jiminy Cricket

The high clouds look like heavy waves that are smashing up against a big pirate ship with torn sails. Evil pirates are being tossed about and thrown into the sea. They cannot escape the demise that they themselves have been guilty of inflicting on so many innocent people.

Nina is lying on her back on the roof of the playhouse, up and away from the reality of the backyard.

Mo interrupts her daydream by calling up to her, "Will you help me fly from the high end of the teeter totter?"

Nina's private adventure ends abruptly.

She tells Mo, "Nobody can fly. Believe me, you will only hurt yourself and go crying to Mommy."

Mo is persistent in her pleading. "Please, P L E A S E! Pretty pretty please! I know you can make me fly!"

Nina does secretly wish that they could fly but would never tell such a thing to her little sister. She is envious of Mo's faith and trust and wonders if just maybe, because Mo really truly believes that she can fly, it might just work if she can launch her high enough into the sky.

The teeter totter, a simple long plank of wood, is balanced on a raised rod. A person sitting on either end can tip the board up and down by virtue of body weight and gravity.

Being the heavier of the two, Nina carefully raises Mo, who is sitting on the opposite end of the board, to the highest point of the teeter totter, and watches her try to stand.

A cautious Mo says, "I can't stand up because the board is too steep. Make it lower."

Nina lowers the board enough for Mo to stand, but that doesn't make Mo happy either. She doesn't think she's high enough off the ground to fly properly, so she gives her big sister even more instructions.

"Bounce up and down – fast – to shoot me into the sky!"

Nina slightly raises her end of the teeter totter, then brings it down to the ground with a hard bump. Mo flies into the air, then crashes face first into the grass. She doesn't cry right away, but only because the fall knocked the wind out of her.

Crumpled, and with blood on her chin and grass stains on her blouse, she gets up and sobs, "You did that on purpose! MOMMY, NINA HURT ME AGAIN!" she wails as she runs to the house.

Nina shouts after her, "WE NEEDED FAIRY DUST!"

The smell from the tank of the sea lions is not so bad this afternoon, but the noise of barking is deafening. Mo shrieks loudly as she gets splashed by a wave of cold, dirty water when a large seal leaps toward her to take the slippery fish from her hand.

Marie scolds her, "If you don't want to get wet, just throw the fish, stupid."

Nina glances across the large tank of seawater and notices a boy that looks about her age, staring at them. She can't help staring back and suddenly realizes where she has seen him before.

"Oh my gosh! Look, Marie! That's the boy I saw yesterday!"

Marie rolls her eyes, makes a hissing noise, and turns her back. When Nina looks again, the boy is gone.

Dad hurries the family away from the sea lions saying, "Time to eat. Our table is ready."

They walk under a bright flashing yellow and blue neon sign of a Chinaman's hat with two fast–moving chopsticks going up and down, up and down, up and down. Nina excitedly asks Dad if his friend is working tonight so they can get extra fortune cookies.

Dinner was uneventful, except that Nina's fortune cookie promised an adventure in the near future. There were no arguments or loud outbursts from Mo. However, what's about to happen at the movie is another story!

Prince Charming on his white horse, carrying the Sword of Truth and the Shield of Honor, cuts through the hundred–year growth of thorny bushes that have grown up around Sleeping Beauty's castle. All of a sudden a scary and LOUD dragon looms up in front of the Prince and breathes a large ball of fire directly at him! The dragon is really the evil witch who transformed herself into a fierce dragon to kill Prince Charming so that he cannot rescue Sleeping Beauty.

Mo cries out, "I DON'T LIKE THAT DRAGON! I WANT TO GO HOME!"

She proceeds to climb over the back of her seat, crawls over the surprised people who are sitting behind the family, and runs up the aisle and out of the theater.

Dad is quick to react and demands, "We are leaving! NOW!"

Both Marie and Nina plead, "Oh, please Daddy, can't we stay? It's almost over!"

The angry audience is making as much noise with their comments of, "Down in front! Be quiet!" And a large unanimous "SHUSH!"

Mom calmly says to Dad, "Now, dear, you go after Mo and I'll stay here with the girls," but he doesn't listen to reason.

"No! We stay together, Get up, now!"

Marie and Nina are in tears as Mom has them get up to leave. Marie sobs, "You don't have to yell at us, Daddy. I've never been so embarrassed in my whole life. I wish that I had stayed home. I hate this family!"

"Are you still mad at me?"

Nina hears Mo's timid voice from under her top bunk. She has been giving her little sister the silent treatment ever since the family left the theater.

Nina breaks her silence. "Why do you have to ruin everything? You act like a baby to get what you want! You will never know if Prince Charming rescued Sleeping Beauty because I won't tell you how it ends!"

"That dragon scared me!" cries Mo.

"How can anybody be scared of a cartoon? Did you think it was for real?"

Mo doesn't reply for fear of ridicule because she really does believe in fairy tales, as well as every made—up story Nina has ever told her. With heavy eyelids, Nina rolls over to hug her pillow and says while yawning, "Go to sleep."

Mo is not about to go to sleep. She is standing in her bottom bunk and looking into Nina's face. "If you were a fairy tale girl, who would you be?"

"I don't know." Nina yawns, turning her face toward the wall.

Mo bounces on her mattress and says in a sing—song voice, "I would be Sleeping Beauty and you would be Cinderella!"

Nina snaps, "I AM Cinderella in this house! Go to sleep!"

"No, you are Cinder*nina*," says Mo.

"Cindernina, Cindernina, all I hear is Cindernina, Cinder, Cinder, Cinder, Nina, Nina, Nina.

Take the trash out, set the table, clear the table, wash the dishes, get to work… Cindernina.”

Nina is impressed as well as surprised that Mo knows her song.

“Okay, Mo. If you really want to know who would I like to be, I'll tell you. I used to want to be Snow White because of the diamond mine, but now I wish I could be Peter Pan's Wendy.”

Mo has stopped bouncing, and with a faraway expression on her face, she says in a hushed voice, “Oh… so you can fly and see fairies and mermaids?”

Nina, who is wide awake now, sits up and begins to tell her favorite ongoing story.

“Peter Pan and Tinkerbell are here right now, but they are invisible to everybody but me. If you get back in bed, I will talk to them and tell you what they say.”

Nina keeps a flashlight and a tiny bell in her bed so she'll always be prepared to continue her saga about Peter Pan and Tinkerbell. She flashes the tiny light about the ceiling while ringing the bell – her own rendition of a fairy's light and twinkling voice. She tells Mo, “Tinkerbell says that she was watching you today when you tried to fly. You made her laugh. Peter says that you might be able to fly if you had fairy dust sprinkled on you.”

An excited Mo, who is stretching her head as far off her bed as possible without falling in an effort to see Peter Pan, says, "Ask him if I can have some fairy dust!"

Nina rings the tiny bell, flashes the light quickly around the room, and tells Mo that Tinkerbell will not share her dust with ANY girl. She laughs and comments, "Peter thinks it's funny that she is jealous of us."

After some thought Mo asks, "Why would Tinkerbell be jealous of us?"

Nina's story is becoming more of a tale of her own secret desire as she replies to her sister, "Because she's afraid Peter will like us better than her, and he might take us to Neverland.

Remember how Tinkerbell was so mean to Wendy? It was because she was jealous of her."

Nina is thinking hard to make up her new story about how to react to a jealous fairy. Her interests have been only for Peter Pan and becoming his new Wendy. Tinkerbell's only importance has always been to provide the needed fairy dust for flying.

She drops the bell while fumbling with the flashlight. Of course, it hits Mo in the middle of her forehead. Mo cries out as she jumps back onto her pillow and pulls the covers over her head,

"YOU TRICKED ME! You made up all the stories about Peter Pan!"

Nina's reply has a hidden meaning for both her and her little sister.

"You are so easy to trick. You know that Peter Pan and Tinkerbell are just make–believe… and Dad is really Santa Claus!"

Marie enters the room, climbs into her bed, and says, "Aren't you brats asleep yet? School starts tomorrow. We have to get up early, so stop talking and go to sleep."

Mo is softly crying. Nina whispers, "I'm sorry I dropped the bell on your head."

But Nina is more sorry that she has ruined Mo's belief in what she herself wishes were a reality. Mo may never again believe in her sister's stories.

CHAPTER FOUR

All you need is faith and trust, and a little bit of pixie dust!

Peter Pan

"Turn it off," Nina groans as she pulls the covers over her head.

Marie is hunting through her musical jewelry box. She always leaves the lid open longer than necessary to annoy her sisters.

"You've always hated my music box. You'd better get up! Mo ran away last night, and Mom is looking for her. You'll have to get ready for school by yourself."

"Mo wouldn't run away in the night. She's afraid of the dark."

Marie is putting on her new flats – the kind of shoes all the high school girls wear.

"Maybe if you had not told her the truth about Peter Pan, Tinkerbell, and Santa Claus, she wouldn't have left."

Nina knows her little sister too well to believe that she wouldn't ran away and says to Marie, "I'll bet she's hiding in the playhouse because she doesn't want to go to school."

But Nina can't help but know how distraught Mo was last night and fears that Mo really has run away. She is mad at herself and worried about Mo.

"I'm leaving now, Nina. I don't want to be late for the first day. I suggest you get dressed and make your lunch."

Marie puts her new tube of Avon lipstick in her purse and reminds Nina, "Remember, I told you that you have to walk to and from school by yourself. Maybe if you put your mind into hurrying you won't be late. As if YOU can do anything in a hurry!"

With that unnecessary remark, Marie picks up the lunch that she made for herself and walks out the front door, slamming it behind her.

The empty house is now very quiet except for the dripping kitchen faucet. Nina slides off her top bunk, hurries through the house, and rushes out the backdoor in hopes of finding Mo in the playhouse.

There is something strangely eerie about the atmosphere in the playhouse. The air inside makes Nina's damp skin tangle. She doesn't notice the substance that sparkles in the cracks of the rough cement floor. Her heart sinks when she sees that Mo is not there.

Closing the front door behind her for the first time in her life gives Nina a sense of responsibility. She is proud of herself for tying the sash on the back of her plaid dress and for making her own lunch, even though neither ordeal was without its trials. After numerous attempts to tie the sash on her dress using the mirror, she finally took the dress off, laid it on the floor, tied a perfect bow, and put it back on.

Opening the can of tuna for her sandwich was not so simple. While turning the key of the can opener, Nina didn't know not to tip the can, and tuna oil spilled down the front of her dress and onto the floor. She used the wet dishcloth to wipe her dress, then finished making her sandwich before pouring milk into her new red plaid thermos that matched her new lunch box and her dress. Finally, she's ready for her first day in the fifth grade!

Sensing that she's late, Nina decides to take the shortcut through the back alleys. She often travels this way because she can go deep within her imagination without being interrupted by well—meaning neighbor ladies who stand in front of their yards. If they saw her today, she could be certain of hearing that she'd better get moving.

Trash cans are overflowing, waiting to be emptied. She kicks another rock in the soft damp soil and notices the dirt on her brand new white saddle oxfords. She had been so careful not to put creases in them of scuff them the night she and her sisters had worn their new shoes out of Sears. She looked funny walking with flat feet and had trouble keeping up with the family. Dad had scolded her, "Walk right!"

To Nina's credit, she did hurry through the first two alleys, but what she is about to discover in the third alley will not only make her late for school but will change her life forever, or at least the way she looks at it.

Loose trash has been spread about by animals, and most of the cans are haphazardly strewn about. The alley looks a mess except for one little area that is swept clean around a small blue wooden shed that contains two blue trash cans. There sitting on the top of the trash, as if waiting to be found, is the most beautiful book that Nina has ever seen. Its cover is adorned with what looks like multicolored glitter, only these sparkles are much richer and brighter than plain glitter. She cannot resist picking up the book and looking inside. Written on the first page in very small, fancy gold print are the words:

"You, the reader, hath been selected to learn the truth within these pages."

With both dread and excitement, Nina turns the page and reads,

THE TRUTH ABOUT FAIRIES

*FAIRIES ARE MAGICAL BEINGS KNOWN TO VISIT CHILDREN
WITH IMAGINATION WHO LIVE IN THE REAL WORLD.*

Nina startles herself as she exclaims loudly, "They are real! I knew it!"

Never in her life has she been so interested in reading a book. She sees a place to sit between the two blue trash cans, wedges herself in, and draws her knees to her chest to make a support for her newly found treasure. The cover of the book mesmerizes her. Each of the twinkling specks of color has its own light. She can't help but stare at them for several minutes before turning the magical pages.

Some of what she reads is the same as what she has already learned from her fairy tale books and movies – like, "A fairy is the size of a baby's fist and looks like a ball of light," and "Because its heart is so small, the fairy has a very short life."

The new information is fascinating.

"Few people are able to see the tiny fairy's figure or hear its tinkling, but the few who do see and hear are chosen to do so."

Nina always pretended that only she could hear what Tinkerbell was saying, but it was just a made–up story for Mo's benefit. Now that she has been chosen to read this book, she is hoping that she will be chosen to see and hear real fairies. And maybe – just maybe – they will share their fairy dust with her so she can fly. That is, if they have dust! She keeps reading to find out.

"Fairies never really die. When their light begins to fade, they go through a regeneration that is much like that of a butterfly. A fairy's light is its internal heat that keeps it alive. As its light fades, it becomes cold and immobile. When that happens, the fairy will fold itself up tightly in its wings and go to sleep until a new internal light grows strong enough for the fairy to burst from its wrapping and begin life again with the same memory and personality."

"Although it rarely happens, there is a way for a fairy to die completely. Death happens only if the fairy becomes wet during its rebirth."

"No wonder Tinkerbell has been around for such a long time," thinks Nina. "This book makes a lot of sense."

She continues reading and learns that fairies come in many colors, but the majority of them are yellow. Yellow fairies are known to be mischievous, possessive, and temperamental. All fairies have internal heat of varying degrees according to their color, with a temper to match their heat. So a red fairy is hot and volatile, a yellow fairy is warm, and a blue fairy is cool and pleasant. There are also a few fairies of orange, green, and lavender temperaments.

"There is only one Blue Fairy. She is kind, understanding, and will not tolerate evil. People have written many stories about her and her magic."

Nina nods her head in acknowledgement as she remembers how the Blue Fairy gave life to the wooden puppet, Pinocchio.

She reads about Red Fairies and how they've been known to become so angry that their heat will make them burn up. They are not welcome in the fairy world because of their deceit and evil deeds. Red Fairies have become rare.

"Much has been said about fairy dust."

Finally! Fairy dust information!

Nina scoots further back in her nook in preparation for finding out what she is dying to know, but the magic is interrupted as the trash truck enters the alley.

BANG! CLANG! ROAR!

Nina flees from her hiding place with her book and lunch in hand. The large sash of her dress catches a piece of metal and tears away, leaving a hole where it had been sewn. Running quickly away from the moving truck, she trips on a rock and falls flat on her stomach, sending her new book and lunch pail flying just as the school bell sounds.

BUZ...Z...Z...Z!

A new stinging pain from her freshly skinned knees shoots through her body to add to the soreness of Saturday's tumble at the tide pools. It doesn't even phase Nina. Her only concern for now is to get to the playground and line up with her class before her new teacher notices that she is late.

CHAPTER FIVE

I close my eyes, then I drift away, into the magic night I softly say
A silent prayer, like dreamers do, then I fall asleep to dream my
dreams of you.

Roy Orbison

The humming of the bees in the bushes that line the chainlink fence go unnoticed by Nina, who **is hiding as she watches her class walk past the flag pole, the auditorium, and into the two-story building. She waits for the playground to clear.**

Now is a perfect chance to play on the rings without having to wait in line or get pushed off the ramp. At the same time, she'd really like to spend a little more time reading the book she's just found. Even though she is stiff and sore, the rings win. She cannot pass up the opportunity of having the rings all to herself.

She has grown over the summer and no longer needs help to reach the first ring above the launching board. Swinging back and forth, a ring in either hand, she lets go of one and catches another in the circle of rings that are suspended on long chains. Round and round she propels herself until the pain of new blisters is too much and she falls flat on her belly into the sand.

Last year, she used the rings so many times that calluses had developed, but her hands softened over the summer, and right now her soft hands burned.

"What do you think you're doing, young lady?"

Nina raises her head to see a pair of feet with bright red painted toes in shiny black patent leather high heels. It's Miss Perete, the principal, whom Nina calls Miss Pirate behind her back. She's wearing a tight red skirt and a tight black fuzzy sweater. She would look just like Mo's Barbie Doll if it weren't for her long black hair.

"Get up and come with me!"

Nina knows she is going to the office – a horrid place that unfortunately she knows too well. She watches the principal walk with quick short steps in her tight skirt.

The seat of the big wide wooden chair is cold on Nina's legs. Her feet stick out straight in front of her, and she notices her dirty new shoes.

Miss Perete wiggles into her swivel chair behind her big desk and says to Nina, "You are a sight. Where did you go before you came to school today? I don't usually see you in my office until the second week of school. Weren't most of those visits to my office before because you were caught playing on the rings after recess was over? What do you think should be your punishment for not going to class this morning?"

Nina is watching the dirt fall from her shoes as she rotates her feet and mumbles, "I don't know… maybe you should send me home?"

With raised eyebrows, Miss Perete leans forward saying, "I think not. Look at me when I talk to you! You look like you've been in a fight."

Nina looks past the principal at a seagull that has perched on the windowsill behind her. Half listening to the principal, she replies, "I wasn't in a fight. I was reading and forgot about school."

The principal is frustrated with Nina's lack of attention and repeats, "Look at me! That book you have is not proper for you to read. I'll take that, thank you."

She leans over her desk and takes the book about fairies from Nina's grasp and places it on her desk. The book is no longer sparkling, but looks old and worn.

Now Nina turns her attention toward the mean woman. She glares at her while thinking to herself, "How dare you take my book, and how would you know if it is unsuitable for children? You were not chosen to read it! I was!"

She stares at the principal and watches Miss Pirate's bright red lips move over her teeth as she describes Nina's numerous visits to her office in the past two years. There is lipstick on her front tooth. She reminds Nina of someone evil. She studies her intently, noticing every detail of the principal's face. The way her long black hair turns under at her shoulders and her mean eyes make Nina think of Captain Hook, the pirate who fought Peter Pan In Neverland. Nina says under her breath, "You ARE Miss Pirate."

"What did you call me? What is wrong with you? Your sister, Marie, NEVER gave me any trouble. Now what do I do with an enigma like you?"

Nina's eyes are on the wooden paddle with holes in it that is hanging on the wall next to the desk. Rumor has it that really bad children have been spanked with that paddle. She wonders if playing on the rings warrants the use of the paddle, but that would really be stupid. It's not like she hurt anybody. She asks, "What's an enigma?"

"An enigma," says Miss Perete, "is someone who is different from anybody else. Your punishment will be no playground activities. You will sit on the lunch benches by yourself during lunch and recess and report to the office twenty minutes before and after school. You will do this for two weeks."

Her words are cutting, making Nina sad because she knows that she is not like the other children. What the principal doesn't realize is that the punishment won't really be hard to take. Nina is used to being by herself.

"Welcome to the 5th grade, Nina! You can sit next to Eugene," says Mrs. Van Luven. Of all the teachers at John Muir Elementary School, Nina's new teacher is the nicest and most liked. Nina knows she is going to enjoy being in her class and has hopes that the rest of the school year will be better than the beginning of the first day.

Eugene, who lives next door, whispers, "I heard about what happened to Mo."

Nina is surprised that anyone could know anything about her family's recent drama and is about to ask what he had heard when a loud buzzing disrupts her inquiry. Mrs. Van Luven calmly says, "Class, this is an air raid drill. Please line up. We will file out of the room slowly and line up in single file against our classroom's wall in the hall."

The hallway is packed with children who are in line against the wall in front of their classrooms. Miss Perete is standing at the far end of the hall near the stairwell. Nina glares at her.

In her commanding voice, Miss Perete instructs, "When I say DUCK AND COVER, I want everyone of you to drop to your knees, put your foreheads on the floor, and clasp your hands over your head. Do so quickly and stay close to the wall."

"DUCK AND COVER!"

Nina is enjoying this weird drill even though the floor and wall are cold and the purpose of this exercise is frightening. She wonders if Miss Perete is on her knees and how she could manage to get down on the floor in her tight skirt. Nina lifts her head and is quickly scolded by the standing principal.

"Nina! Put your head down!"

Eugene says, "The principal doesn't like you, does she?"

Because the drill took up so much time, the students are released immediately afterward to the playground, and Nina to the lunch benches. The thirty minutes of punishment pass quickly for Nina, who passes much of the time peeling large strips of worn paint off the bench. She is feeling guilty about being mean to Mo and hopes that Mom has found her.

Another bell rings, and back to class everyone goes. Mrs. Van Luven is teaching fractions by drawing a large chocolate pie on the chalkboard.

She is cutting it in half, then in fourths, and then in eighths. Nina finally understands fractions and is pleased with herself for keeping up with the class. It's already lunchtime, and so far class has been fun.

A seagull lands at the end of the lunch bench. He is attracted to the strong smell of tuna fish coming from Nina's open lunch box.

"Are you my Seagully?" she asks the bird as he sidesteps closer to her lunch.

He grabs the sandwich with his beak and flies to the middle of the bench, devouring his oily treat in three big gulps.

"You are my Seagully!" Nina excitedly exclaims. She is so happy that her best friend has found her. "I really need to talk to you."

But she loses the opportunity to tell him her story because he flies away when a boy comes running toward the lunch benches waving his arms and shouting.

"LOOK! A SEAGULL!"

Coachie, the ever present playground supervisor, blows her whistle at the boy and shouts for all to hear, "That young lady is being disciplined. Stay away from her."

The remainder of the school day isn't any better. Nina's eyes are glued to the big clock on the wall, hearing as well as seeing every tick of its big hand.

Finally, the minute hand ticks to three-thirty and the loud bell rings. But school is not yet over for her until she does her time in the office.

Nobody seems to know why she is sitting by herself in Miss Perete's office. After thirty minutes she is asked to leave. Her book is nowhere to be seen.

The walk home is slow and full of contemplation for Nina. Having lost possession of the book about fairies angers her. She rarely gets mad and is upset by her feelings of revenge toward Miss Perete.

She purposely steps on every crack in the sidewalk and chants, "Step on a crack and break Perete's back."

"Why would she even want a book she hasn't read? Does she know what's in the book? I never got to the part about fairy dust!"

Nina must find a way to get it back.

The house is dark and quiet. Mom is not in the kitchen, there is no dinner waiting, no Marie, and no Mo. She takes the heavy glass gallon bottle of milk from the icebox and slips on the fish oil she had spilled that morning while making her lunch. Down she goes, and the full bottle of milk shatters as it hits the floor.

Nina breaks into uncontrollable sobs and yells, "This is the worst day of my life!"

She carefully picks up the chunks and shards of glass and sops up the large puddle and splatters of milk with the two fresh bath towels she retrieves from the bathroom.

Thinking that her favorite TV show will make her feel better, she turns it on, only to hear the very last notes of the closing song,

"M...O...U...S...EEE"

She has long wished to be a Mouseketeer. She even has her own official ears and club shirt with her name on it that she got on her last birthday at Disneyland.

The living room is draped in blue shadows from the light of the TV. Nina turns it off.

"I hate being alone! Where is everybody?"

Dad always comes home at six–thirty on the dot, and she is hoping that he will be here before too long. She turns on every light in the house and takes a much needed bath. Unfortunately, she used the last two bath towels in the kitchen, so she dries herself with her favorite blue nightgown before putting it on. Climbing onto her top bunk, she curls up under the covers and cries herself to sleep.

Nina sleeps like she is floating in deep water and cannot catch her breath. Her mind is full of sadness. She releases it to go where it will.

The loud screeching of a seagull wakes her with a start. It sounds as if the bird is just outside her bedroom window. She slides off her top bunk to open it. Nina is positive that her seagull friend has come to see her. The low window is not easy to raise, but she manages to get it open wide enough to look down into the garden below. Strange. The plants have some sort of glitter on them. But where is her seagull friend?

Nina is half hanging out the window staring at the ground when suddenly she senses someone standing in front of her — so close that she bumps his chest as she cautiously raises her head.

"YOU!" says Nina, who is looking into the smiling eyes of the boy she had met at Cabrillo Beach.

"Everyone else always leaves the window open for me."

Printed in the USA
CPSIA information can be obtained
at www.ICGtesting.com
LVHW080735220324
774975LV00023B/237